HOME BEFORE
THE RAVEN CAWS

HOME BEFORE THE RAVEN CAWS

The Mystery of Indiana's Alaskan Totem Pole

RICHARD D. FELDMAN

GUILD PRESS
EMMIS BOOKS

Published in association with
The Eiteljorg Museum of American Indians and Western Art

GUILD PRESS / EMMIS BOOKS
40 Monument Circle
Indianapolis, Indiana 46204

ISBN 1-57860-126-6
Library of Congress Control Number 2003102902

Frontespiece
Painting of the Eiteljorg Museum totem pole raising by Jane McGovern, from the collection of Marki and Rachel Sentany.

The pen and ink drawings on pages 7–11 are by JoAnn George. The photos in this book, unless otherwise designated, were taken by or are courtesy of the author, Richard Feldman.

Cover design by Steven D. Armour
Interior and text design by Sheila G. Samson

Dedicated to

Mary Yeltatzie Swanson and Lee Wallace . . .

and to the memory of

Edwin DeWitt,
Priscilla Rubincam,
Wayne Shields,
Max Parry,
and Mary Freeda Parry . . .

whose lives were touched by a totem pole.

PREFACE

At the Eiteljorg Museum of American Indians and Western Art stands a magnificent totem pole. This pole re-creates a totem pole that once stood in the Indianapolis neighborhood of Golden Hill. Visitors often ask about the pole's history and about the story it tells. Finding answers to those questions involved a true modern-day adventure.

Solving the historical mystery of the once lost and forgotten totem pole and the project to have the pole re-created was a journey that took me across the continent and back in time more than a century. Through this experience, I made many warm friendships with people who had some type of connection with the old pole, with individuals who shared my passion to see a new pole raised, and with Haida and Tlingit natives from Alaska and British Columbia. It was indeed an experience of a lifetime!

Now you are invited to come along on a journey to discover the story of the Golden Hill totem pole—and all the people whose hearts and lives were part of it.

Richard D. Feldman
December 2002

Traditional pole raising at the Eiteljorg Museum, April 13, 1996. (Courtesy Shawn Spence)

ACKNOWLEDGMENTS

I wish to express my appreciation to the following individuals who provided their assistance in the development of this book: Fran Feldman; my wife, Becky Feldman; and Cathy Burton, education manager at the Eiteljorg Museum, gave valuable editorial suggestions. Sherry Hamstra, reading arts teacher at The Orchard School in Indianapolis, provided careful evaluation of the manuscript's reading level. I am most appreciative for the assistance provided by Gail Peterson and other individuals at the Southeast Alaska Indian Cultural Center, Sitka, Alaska, and JoAnn George of Angoon, Alaska, for their cultural review of the material presented.

Thanks also to Lee Wallace, Ketchikan, Alaska, for his knowledgeable contributions; Gene Griffin, Mitzi Frank, Sue Thorsen, and Marieke Van Damme at Sitka National Historical Park; Dan Savard at the Royal British Columbia Museum; and George Miles at the Beinecke Library, Yale University, for their assistance; Tom Krasean at the Indiana Historical Society; John and Jeanette Vanausdall, James Nottage, Dru Doyle, Steve Sipe, Cindy Dashnaw, and Ray Gonyea at the Eiteljorg Museum for their involvement; and Nancy Baxter, Guild Press Emmis Books, for her encouragement and guidance.

My sincerest gratitude extends to Bill Holm, curator emeritus of Northwest Coast art at the Burke Museum and professor emeritus of art history at the University of Washington for his factual review of the manuscript and for his help in photographically identifying the original Golden Hill totem pole in Alaska. Finally, I wish to acknowledge Dr. Judith Scherer, who helped guide the latter aspects of my research and whose contributions assisted in the tracing of the Golden Hill totem pole to its Native Alaskan origins.

The Haida village of Skidegate, Alaska, Queen Charlotte Islands, 1881.
(Courtesy British Columbia Archives, neg. # G 00120)

WHAT IS A TOTEM POLE?

TOTEM POLES are created only by the native coastal peoples of the Pacific Northwest. These large wood carvings, made from red western cedar trees that grow in the forests of this region, vary in size, but can be as tall as sixty feet.

Totem poles consist of figures of animals, birds, fish, plants, insects, humans, and elements of nature such as the moon and sun, along with supernatural beings. Large interlocking figures, one on top of another, make up the main body of the pole. Smaller figures are positioned in the spaces between these larger characters, and are tucked inside their ears, or hang out of their mouths. They are both artistic and interesting.

Totem poles are not religious objects, but they are very important in the culture of these native peoples and communicate information to the observer. Most totem poles tell a story about an important event, person, legend, or mythical history of the family that owns the pole. Most of the animals and other characters carved on the pole are part of the story the totem represents.

Many of these totem pole stories involve animals because, as with all Native American groups, the native peoples of the Northwest Coast have great respect for animals. Animals are observed carefully because the people believe that each animal possesses specific spiritual qualities and importance. Wisdom, power, and success can be gained by understanding them and by properly treating the animal spirits. For these reasons, family stories establishing a family connection with certain animals affirm the importance of the owner's heritage. For instance, some stories may characterize the clan's mythical ancestors who, long ago, had supernatural experiences with animals or other beings. Or a clan may trace its history to an animal that changed into a human and established the beginning of the family. A totem pole is a living storybook that reinforces the family's history and sense of pride.

The map on the facing page shows the native cultural groups of the Northwest Coast. (Map by Steve Sipe)

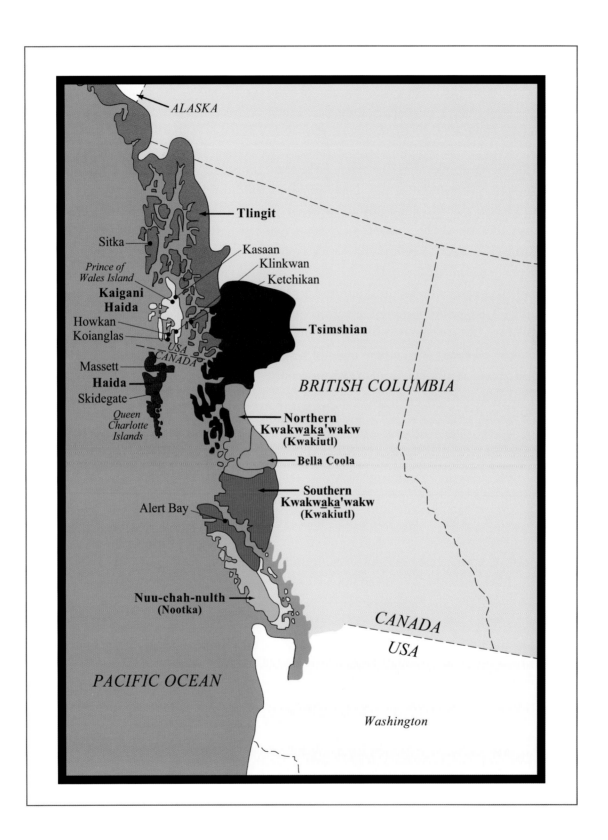

WHO MAKES TOTEM POLES?

THE NATIVE PEOPLES OF THE PACIFIC NORTHWEST COAST

THE NATIVE peoples who have totem poles have very similar, yet different, cultures and also speak different languages. These people include the Haida, Tlingit, Tsimshian, Kwakwaka'wakw (Kwakiutl), Bella Coola, and Nuu-chah-nulth (Nootka). They live in a region of islands and coastal areas of southeastern Alaska and British Columbia, Canada. These native groups use the sea as a source of food and catch fish, especially salmon and halibut, shellfish, and other sea animals, including sea lions and whales. They also gather nuts, berries, roots, and vegetables as well as hunt small land animals. Because their environment is rich in food and other natural resources, they have a great deal of time for art and other ways of expressing their social and cultural values. They are known for their art of wood carving, which in addition to totem poles includes carved boxes, masks, rattles, bowls, clubs, spoons, and canoes.

Totem poles are important to the family group structure in the Pacfic Northwest. The Haida, Tlingit, and Tsimshian each separate themselves into two or more major divisions called "moieties." Each Haida person belongs to either the raven or the eagle moiety. The moieties are further divided into more closely related family groups called clans. Traditionally, several families within a clan lived together in a large clan house. A totem pole typically stood proudly outside the house.

Unlike many other Native American groups, those of the Northwest Coast in traditional times had a system of social rank based mostly on wealth and power. Social status was a very important part of the culture and way of life of these native groups. Their lives were entirely centered around the village, and the clan leaders and their oldest nephews enjoyed the highest status in the community and were considered as royalty. (A male child was sent to live with and be raised by his mother's brother. He was treated like a son and inherited his uncle's position and wealth). Younger nephews, brothers, and other closely related family members of the clan leaders followed this group in rank as nobility. Of lower status were the common people who worked as craftsmen, tradesmen, and fishermen. Slaves were at the lowest social level. These people, taken captive in wars, were the servants of the clan leaders and their families.

Totem poles were very expensive to have carved. Because of that, they were one of the best symbols of a family's power and social status.

Shared Symbols
How the Totem Pole Tells a Story

But what is the meaning of a totem pole? Totem poles cannot be read like a book. They can be understood only by someone who knows the myth or story behind the pole, since the carved figures are merely symbols for the major characters or events in the story. Some of the stories represented by the poles are so well-known by the native people that they can understand the entire story that is carved on the pole. In this case, when particular characters are placed together on a totem pole, they become recognized as a group and become a shared symbol of the mythical legend that the pole tells. If a story is not well-known, a person looking at the pole knows only that certain animals are included, but not the specific story.

Some figures on the pole may not be part of the story but are present simply to fill up space. Other figures, such as the raven or the eagle, which indicate the moiety to which the pole's owner belongs, may be included at the top of the pole. Animal characters representing the clan, such as the wolf, bear, frog, or killer whale, may be included in the carving as well.

By the consistent use of certain characteristics of the animals over time (although each native group has a slightly different carving style), carvers also developed a system of shared symbols that allowed people to recognize one animal from another. The raven always has a long, straight beak, while the eagle has a curved beak. The beaver has two large front teeth or a piece of wood held in both paws. The bear always has a mouth full of big, sometimes pointed teeth, and the killer whale has a large dorsal fin. The wolf has a long, narrow snout, pointed ears, and sharp teeth. Supernatural beings include the thunderbird. It looks much like an eagle but its beak may be more rounded, and it has two feathered, curved "horns" projecting from the top of the head. The sea monster takes on various forms, including that of a wolf-like animal. Frequently, too, the sea monster is an animal with large, oval eyes and a long, rounded-off snout. Watchman figures are humanlike, supernatural beings with very tall hats, which are signs of high status. Although most animals on totem poles are carved as symbolic representations, some, like fish and frogs, are carved more realistically. They look like the animals they're supposed to represent.

Native American myths of the Northwest Coast typically include animals that can transform themselves into other animals, human beings, or other forms. For that reason, totem characters can sometimes be seen as combinations of different animals, or part animal and part human.

Totem poles are complicated artistic and cultural forms. That's what makes them so interesting.

EAGLE (Haida)

RAVEN (Haida)

BEAVER (Haida)

BEAR (Haida)

KILLER WHALE (Tlingit)

FROG (Haida/Tlingit)

WATCHMAN (Haida)

WOLF (Tlingit)

THUNDERBIRD
    (Kwakw<u>a</u>k<u>a</u>'wakw) (Kwakiutl)

TYPES OF TOTEM POLES

OF COURSE, not all totem poles are alike. There are six basic types, each made for a specific purpose. No matter what the particular use, though, all totem poles have great meaning and importance and add beauty as well as a sense of family pride and identity to the lives of the people who own them.

The most familiar type of totem pole among the Northwest Coast peoples is the *house* or *house frontal* pole, the largest and most decorative totem pole. These poles stand outside near, or attached to, the clan house of the most important village leaders. Often, watchman figures are carved at the top to watch over and protect the family and the village. These totem poles are also known as *heraldic*, *crest*, or *family* poles because they are carved with animal figures, or crests, that tell the mythical story of the family or clan that owns the pole.

A special type of house frontal pole is the *entrance* or *doorway* pole. Attached to the center front, it has an oval hole cut through the base that serves as a doorway into the clan house.

Another type of pole, the *house post*, actually supports the roof beams of the large clan houses. These groups of interior posts are usually shorter than many of the exterior poles and are often carved with a large notch at the top for the beam to rest upon. Like the house frontal poles, these house posts are often carved with animal figures such as bears, beavers, ravens, and human figures that tell the mythical stories of the family history. Depending on the particular native group, there can be from two to four or more house posts in a clan house.

Both the Haida and Tlingit have the *mortuary* pole, erected at the death of an important individual. This pole can be carved very plainly with a single figure at the top, but is usually carved over its entire length. The ashes or body of the person the totem honors rests within the top portion of the pole. A *memorial* pole typically stands in front of the clan house and also honors a person who has died. Traditionally, the memorial pole is simply carved with one figure at the top, but may also have an additional figure at the bottom with a large, uncarved space in between. This type of pole is raised about a year after the death of an important person by the relative who is taking over his position in the clan and community. The pole honors the dead individual, but also announces the new successor's position. The figures on the mortuary and memorial poles are important symbols in the personal or family history of the person who has died.

Carved mainly by the Kwakwaka'wakw (Kwakiutl) and the Nuu-chah-nulth (Nootka), the *welcome* pole is a very large, friendly looking single human figure that stands invitingly on the village beach for the purpose of welcoming guests to the community.

The last type of totem pole is the *ridicule* or *shame* pole. It is erected to embarrass a person who owes a debt or has done something to make the owner of the pole very angry. Often, a carving that looks like the person to be shamed appears on the pole. The pole is taken down when the debt is paid or the wrong is corrected.

ABOVE: Author Feldman and his wife, Becky, sitting in the portal entrance to a Tlingit clan house, Totem Bight State Park, Ketchikan, Alaska.

LEFT: Another view of the park's Tlingit clan house, showing the entire entrance type of house frontal pole.

Saanaheit pole and house posts, Sitka National Historical Park, Sitka, Alaska. This house frontal pole is more than fifty feet tall. Saanaheit was a clan leader in the Haida village of Kasaan. (Courtesy Sitka National Historical Park Archives)

Yaadaas crest pole, Sitka National Historical Park, Sitka, Alaska. This Haida house frontal pole is from the village of Kasaan. The pole's bear and the raven characters are crest figures of the Yaadaas clan. (Courtesy Sitka National Historical Park Archives)

Haida house posts, Kasaan, ca. 1903. (Courtesy Yale Collection of Western Americana, Beinecke Rare Book and Manuscript Library)

A clan house in the Haida village of Klinkwan stands in ruins around its remaining interior house post, ca. 1902. The top figure is a bear. (Courtesy of the Royal British Columbia Museum, Victoria, British Columbia. neg # PN 160)

Haida mortuary poles (center and left), Queen Charlotte Islands, ca. 1880.
(Courtesy British Columbia Archives neg # G 03548)

A raven figure perches atop this Tlingit memorial pole in Sitka National Historical Park. (Courtesy Sitka National Historical Park Archives)

A villager huddles near a Kwakwa̲ka'wakw (Kwakiutl) welcome figure, Alert Bay, British Columbia, ca. 1900. (Courtesy Yale Collection of Western Americana, Beinecke Rare Book and Manuscript Library)

The Trader Legend Pole in Sitka National Historical Park is an example of a ridicule pole. The top figure represents a white man, possibly a trader who cheated the Haida. Below the man's head are the figures of a shrimp and a crab, both symbols of a thief. (Courtesy Sitka National Historical Park Archives)

Carving a Totem Pole

Native peoples of the Pacific Northwest have probably been carving totem poles for several hundred years. The first tools used to carve totem poles were made of stone, shell, or bone. They were more difficult to work with than the iron tools brought by white traders by both land and sea in the late 1700s. Until the natives had iron tools to use, the carving of totem poles was a very slow and difficult process. For that reason, early poles were probably smaller and simpler in design than those produced beginning in the middle of the nineteenth century. Totem-pole carving was a profession for only the most skilled artists, who would be hired by important individuals in the villages who desired a pole.

The red western cedar tree is used for poles because it's a soft, easily carved, lightweight wood that is naturally somewhat weather- and insect-resistant. A tree for a totem pole is carefully selected for straightness, diameter, height, and a lack of lower branches that would create knots in the trunk when removed, thus making carving more difficult. Once the tree is cut down, the branches and the top of the tree are removed. In the old days, the tree would be floated to the site for carving. Today, a log that weighs several tons is transported by boat or barge from its island site in Alaska or

Canada, and then brought to the carving site by truck. There, the carver and his assistants strip off the bark and cut away the outer layers of wood, known as sapwood. Nowadays this is often accomplished by planing the tree trunk with large chain saws. Next, the side of the tree to be carved is chosen, and the back half of the tree is removed. The center of the log is then hollowed out, resulting in a crescent-shaped, half-round log. This hollowing out lightens the log and prevents cracking of the wood as it dries.

In the old days, the basic outlines of the figures would be painted on the wood to guide the carving, but much of the work was done freehand. Today, carvers usually create paper patterns and place them on the pole so they can outline the design to be carved. Chain saws make initial rough shapes and certain cuts so the later carving is easier. Additional work is done with chopping tools of various sizes called adzes, and with chisels. The finer details are created with knives and other small woodworking tools.

Finally, the pole is painted, but only to highlight certain details of the figures. Originally, paints were made from materials found in nature, and mixed with the liquid part of salmon eggs so they would adhere better to the wood. Today, carefully matched commercial paints are used to re-create the old traditional colors.

No matter how the work was done two hundred years ago or how it is done today, the carving of a totem pole combines cultural heritage, art, and satisfaction in crafting work well done.

Raising a Totem Pole

AFTER THE artful crafting of a totem pole is completed, the pole must be placed in the ground so it can be viewed and appreciated. The traditional method for raising a totem pole is to first dig a trench and place the bottom of the pole in it. The other end of the pole is supported at an angle by a wooden framework. Upright wooden boards are placed in the trench for the totem pole to press against as it is raised to an upright position. The pole is raised by many people pulling on ropes tied to the upper end of the pole. The pulling and tugging is directed by a respected individual experienced in raising totem poles, who gives the command for each tug of the ropes. Little by little, the totem pole is lifted to a standing position as members of the native community sing in celebration. Once the pole is upright, the trench is filled with rocks and then dirt. Holding their adzes, the carver and his assistant carvers and other invited individuals then perform the carver's dance around the pole in celebration. The mythical story of the pole is told to everyone, and people give speeches praising the owners.

After the pole raising, the owners of the pole give a "potlatch" event. The potlatch combines feasting, dancing, storytelling, speech-making, and gift-giving. Potlatches are given not only for totem pole raisings but also for other important occasions such as marriages, the naming of a child, or the assuming of new leadership positions in the community. Traditionally, the potlatch was more than a social gathering or a celebration of a particular event. It was an occasion for an important person or a leader of a clan to display his status and wealth. The grander the event and gifts were, the more honor and respect were gained by the hosts. The splendid totem pole that now stood in front of the clan house for all to see was proof of that house's greatness, wealth, and importance.

In the old days, there was no attempt to preserve totem poles. The most important time in the life of the pole was during the pole raising and as the center of attention at the potlatch that followed. Totem poles typically lasted sixty to eighty years, quickly rotting in the humidity of the rain forests of the Pacific Northwest. As the owners wished, new poles were carved to replace the original ones.

THE MYSTERIOUS GOLDEN HILL TOTEM POLE

A forgotten Indianapolis landmark and the missing pole from the Brady Collection of Sitka National Historical Park

ALTHOUGH MOST totem poles remained where they were originally placed, some came to be noticed and admired by non-natives. These special specimens were moved to other places, and sometimes became part of another culture.

At the turn of the twentieth century, in what is now the Indianapolis neighborhood of Golden Hill was the estate of David M. Parry. It was here that a magnificent thirty-foot nineteenth-century totem pole once stood, admired by three generations of Indianapolis residents. By the time I had become curious about the totem pole, and later on when the Eiteljorg Museum of American Indians and Western Art had taken an interest in re-creating it, the pole was gone. Only its stone and concrete foundation on "Totem Lane" remained. For more than ten years we attempted to reconstruct its history. We finally traced the pole's path from Alaska to St. Louis to Indianapolis, and at last the full story could be told.

The story begins with Mr. Parry. He was a nationally known businessman and the owner of the Parry Manufacturing Company of Indianapolis. At one time, it was the largest wagon and carriage company in the world and one of America's early manufacturers of the automobile. Parry held many important business positions, including the presidency of the National Association of Manufacturers. He became one of the most powerful men in America and was even considered a possible vice presidential candidate for Theodore Roosevelt in 1904.

During the time Parry was building his mansion on his wooded Golden Hill estate, the 1904 World's Fair—the Louisiana Purchase Centennial Exposition—was underway in St. Louis, Missouri. Alaska's Governor John Brady (who by coincidence spent part of his boyhood on a farm near Tipton, Indiana, and attended Waveland Collegiate Institute near Crawfordsville) had collected fifteen old totem poles for display at the fair from the native villages on the coastal islands of southeast Alaska in 1903.

Having a sincere respect and concern for Alaska's native peoples, Brady collected these poles and other artifacts in an attempt to preserve their art. He feared that their traditional culture was coming to a end, as the natives were rapidly adopting the white man's way of life. He was particularly concerned about the loss of their totem poles, which were rotting in the humid rain forests of this area of Alaska.

Native peoples didn't often allow their treasured clan poles to be taken away. But Brady was successful in obtaining these poles because native leaders trusted and greatly admired him. They knew him well as a church missionary and governor. Many collectors and museums failed in their efforts to buy totem poles from the same natives who later gave the poles to Brady.

Governor Brady promised the native owners of the poles that he would preserve their totems in a park to be established in Alaska, but first he sent the totem poles to the St. Louis World's Fair. In order to attract fair visitors, he wanted the Alaska pavilion to have an unusual appearance and stand out from the many other attractions. The poles, standing outside the Alaska building along with two authentic native houses on either side, would stop people in their tracks! Brady hoped ultimately to interest people in moving to Alaska and developing businesses there, so that Alaska could be considered for statehood.

Brady placed fourteen of the fifteen poles outside the Alaska building as planned. Because one of the poles had broken, it was thought to be unusable and was piled in a heap alongside the building. "Captain" Dick Crane, who owned the Esquimau Village exhibit at the fair, asked Brady for permission to use the broken pole during the fair.

Crane was an interesting and colorful individual, a dashing adventurer and explorer. In Alaska, he was a steamboat captain on the Yukon River, a trapper, a miner, and trader. He also operated "Dick's Last Chance Trading Post" during the 1898 Klondike Gold Rush, when thousands of Americans and others rushed to Alaska to "strike it rich." After his Alaskan adventures, Captain Dick gathered a group of Alaskan Eskimos and traveled the world. They performed at Madison Square Garden in New York City, at the Coliseum in Chicago, at the Crystal Palace in London, and at other world's fairs displaying their Esquimau Village.

The Esquimau Village at the St. Louis Fair was located along what was known as the Pike. It was a street more than a mile in length, lined with private attractions requiring special admission fees. Crane was able to fix the pole Brady had discarded by recarving or replacing parts of the pole. He used it during the fair in a part of his exhibit called the Klondike mining camp. It included log cabins, a group of Eskimos, native huts, dogs and sled, and mining equipment. The huge Alaskan totem pole stood at the center. It was this pole that became separated from the other Brady-collected poles and eventually found its way to Indianapolis.

When the fair concluded, all but two of the Brady totem poles were returned to Alaska as Brady had promised. These thirteen poles now stand in Sitka National Historical Park in southeast Alaska and became the well-known Brady collection of totem poles. It is one of the most famous groups of totem poles anywhere in the world.

Evidently because the Alaskan government could not afford to ship all the poles back to Alaska, Brady sold the remaining two. He sold one to the Milwaukee Public Museum, and, like the thirteen poles that returned to Alaska, this pole is well-known and accounted for. But the fate and identity of the fifteenth and last pole that ended up in Indianapolis had always been a mystery to historians. Brady sold this damaged pole, once loaned to Dick Crane, to Russell E. Gardner, owner of the Banner Buggy Company in St. Louis and a good friend of David Parry. Gardner then gave the pole to Parry even though the latter did not want it. However, because Parry's son Maxwell became fascinated with the pole, it was erected on the Parry property in Indianapolis in 1905.

Young Max Parry loved the pole and cared for it year after year. In May of 1914, Max wrote that the pole was so old and rotten that he predicted it would not stand another five years. He put the prediction in a bottle, and placed it on top of the pole addressed to the "next poor soul that climbs up here" to repair and paint it. In 1915, about the time of David Parry's death, the Parry family subdivided their estate into a neighborhood they also called Golden Hill. The Indianapolis newspapers advertised Golden Hill lots for sale in a parklike setting, "under the great totem," which stood on a grassy area between the roads. Max's prediction turned out to be quite wrong. The pole would stand in Golden Hill another twenty-five years.

The totem pole became an Indianapolis landmark where children would meet to play, and where young couples would stop to talk. Motorists would come to admire this "Indian" creation with its marvelous carvings on Sunday afternoon drives. There were great discussions regarding the symbolic meaning of the strange carved figures and the pole's history. Although the pole was carved in the mid-nineteenth century, it was generally thought by the Parry family and local residents to be a thousand years old.

The pole continued to stand until the spring of 1939, when, rotten from years of weather and termite attacks, it fell face-down in a storm. Neighborhood children pulled off pieces of the totem pole to keep as souvenirs. The pole was removed and donated to The Children's Museum of Indianapolis by the Parry family in the hopes that it would be repaired and displayed on the museum's front lawn. What actually happened to the pole after its arrival at the museum is a mystery, but it was never displayed and must have been thrown away. In time, the totem pole was almost totally forgotten. No part of the totem pole is known to exist today.

What was the tale the totem pole depicted? It told the story of Wasgo, the sea monster, whose tale can be found in the last chapter of this book.

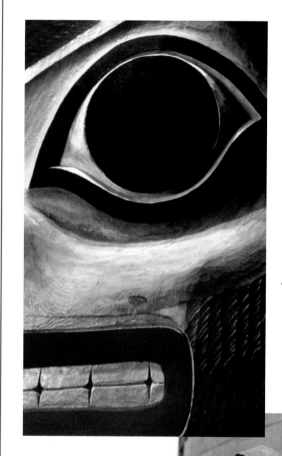

Two close-ups of the Eiteljorg pole—

The bear figure. (Courtesy the Eiteljorg Museum)

And the watchman. (Courtesy Shawn Spence)

Indianapolis businessman David M. Parry received the totem pole as a gift—a gift he did not want. It is unclear why a totem pole, of all things, was chosen as the gift.

John G. Brady was raised in Indiana, educated at Yale University and was appointed governor of Alaska by President William McKinley in 1897. Brady secured what would become the Golden Hill totem pole near Prince of Wales Island in 1903.

"Captain" Dick Crane, owner of the Esquimau Village, used the totem pole on loan from Governor Brady during the 1904 St. Louis World's Fair. A showman and adventurer, he was the "Buffalo Bill Cody" of the Pacific Northwest.

The Alaska Pavilion at the 1904 St. Louis World's Fair (a view of the east side at the top, and the west side below). Governor John Brady displayed fourteen poles outside the building to attract fair visitors. The building contained many examples of Alaska's natural wonders.

The Golden Hill totem pole was displayed at Dick Crane's Esquimau Village at the 1904 St. Louis World's Fair. Visitors did not seem bothered by the blending of the quite separate Eskimo and Northwest Coast Native American cultures.

The exterior of the Esquimau Village was designed to resemble a huge iceberg.

Alaska Governor John Brady (at near center, with white beard) at Alaska Day at the St. Louis World's Fair, October 18, 1904. "Captain" Dick Crane stands on the front row, far right, with his Alaskan Eskimos. (Courtesy Yale Collection of Western Americana, Beinecke Rare Book and Manuscript Library)

The Golden Hill totem pole, Indianapolis, Indiana, ca. 1907. The pole was an Indianapolis landmark for more than thirty years. It has now been identified as the missing pole from the Brady collection of Sitka National Historical Park.

This 1901 photograph shows the Golden Hill totem pole at its original location in the Haida village of Koianglas in southeast Alaska. Alaska Governor John Brady removed the pole from this site in 1903. (Courtesy of National Anthropological Archives, Smithsonian Institution neg. # 92-7098)

SOLVING THE MYSTERY
The Search for the Origins of the Golden Hill Totem Pole

BUT HOW did we do it? How did we find the parts of this puzzle and put them together? Although I am a physician, I also studied Native American art, religion, and culture for two years at Indiana University. I have maintained a keen interest in this field since my college days. Still, I never imagined that I would set out on a ten-year quest to determine the history of a totem pole. But like other paths in life, this one did not open to me until a certain moment. That moment was when we bought a home in the Indianapolis neighborhood of Golden Hill in 1985.

I wondered why our street was called Totem Lane. It seemed like a strange name for an Indianapolis street. Neighbors soon informed me that an authentic totem pole had actually once stood there, and I was shown the stone-and-concrete foundation that remains on the site. I became fascinated with the idea that a totem pole actually stood on Totem Lane. I asked longtime residents of the neighborhood what they remembered about the pole. What they told me was quite simple. They said (as mentioned earlier in this book) that Golden Hill founder David Parry received an Alaskan totem pole as a gift when the 1904 St. Louis World's Fair ended. I searched for information about the pole in local archives and libraries and interviewed everyone I could find who remembered it. I found little information about the pole and no photographs. But I did discover one important thing: I found a 1938 newspaper article about the pole that amazingly agreed with the bits of history told by my neighbors. The article reported that the pole was left behind at the fair by the Alaskan government, and was later given to Mr. Parry by a group of St. Louis businessmen because he was the president of the National Association of Manufacturers.

Several years went by and still I had few answers. I finally wrote to the Missouri Historical Society requesting photographs of the totem poles at the 1904 St. Louis World's Fair. They sent me a number of photographs of fourteen totem poles standing outside the Alaska pavilion and one photograph of a pole at the Esquimau Village exhibit (see page 33). But which one was our Golden Hill pole? Older residents to whom I showed the photographs had only vague memories of the pole and could not identify it. More than one person from this group told me, "If you've seen one totem pole, you've seen them all!"

The quest continued, and I spent the next two years searching for a local photograph of the totem pole. I realized that my search for the totem pole could go no further until I found a photograph of it as it had stood in Golden Hill. Then, quite by chance, an Indianapolis doctor, John MacDougall, overheard me talking about the Golden Hill totem pole. He said his mother (who was nearly a hundred years old) lived near Golden Hill as a young woman. He agreed to look through his mother's old family photographs for one of the totem pole. He found a picture of the old pole taken in Golden Hill about 1914. When I compared this totem pole with the poles at the world's fair, it exactly matched the one displayed at the Esquimau Village! I had actually proven that this authentic totem pole was from the 1904 World's Fair. But had it originally been one of the Brady-collected poles from Alaska? And was it the missing and fifteenth pole from the Brady collection?

A while later, Judith Scherer, an Alaskan anthropologist, contacted me. She was working at Sitka National Historical Park and was tracing the histories of the fifteen Brady poles. Together, we worked for the next eighteen months attempting to prove the Golden Hill totem pole was one of the original Alaskan Brady poles. Had he actually given the pole to Dick Crane at the Esquimau Village, thus starting it on its way to Golden Hill? I needed to prove connections between these two men. I finally decided I needed to go to Yale University to look through the collected letters and other documents of Governor Brady.

In October of 1993 I traveled to Yale and spent two days looking through hundreds of photographs and letters. Two letters (one found at Yale) proved that Brady had indeed loaned the pole to Crane. The letters also provided the necessary information to trace the pole to its original native owner and village. The letters said the pole had originally been donated to Brady by a well-known Haida man named Yeltatzie. And yes, the pole had broken into several pieces. Brady had loaned it to Crane, who repaired it for use at the Esquimau Village. After the fair Brady sold the pole for a hundred and twenty-five dollars to the Banner Buggy Company of St. Louis. So the letters said.

Looking through old Parry family scrapbooks, I saw that Russell E. Gardner, who owned the Banner Buggy Company, was an old friend of David Parry. That was it—he had given the pole to Parry and, as we knew, Parry put it up for his son in Golden Hill.

PRESENTED to Mr. D. M. Parry by the Governor of Missouri, this Indian Totem Pole came from Alaska and is said to be more than one-thousand years old.

Although the Golden Hill totem pole was carved in the middle of the nineteenth century, the Parry family thought the pole was more than a thousand years old, as this page from a 1919 advertising pamphlet for the new Golden Hill neighborhood shows. Still, it shows the pole as it stood in the Indianapolis neighborhood, and that others in addition to Russell Gardner were involved in the transfer of the totem pole to Parry.

The Eiteljorg Museum totem pole. (Courtesy Dan Axler)

Indiana's Alaskan Totem Pole Reborn

The Eiteljorg Museum Totem Pole Project

IT WAS sad to think that this totem pole, which had come so far and meant so much to people over so many years, was now gone and forgotten. It had stood for years, had rotted, fallen down, and then was donated to a museum, where it was lost. It begged to be reborn! If all who heard the story of the Golden Hill totem pole had been thrilled by its mystery, think of how thousands of visitors at a museum would enjoy it! So, in 1991 I established the Eiteljorg Museum Totem Pole Project. Its purpose was to re-create the historic pole and raise it again in Indianapolis. When this was accomplished, the Brady collection of totem poles would be complete once more, and a forgotten Indianapolis landmark would again exist for all to enjoy and appreciate.

The first step was to hire a Haida totem pole carver to re-create the old Kaigani (Alaskan Haida) house frontal totem pole. With the help of Bill Holm—who is one of the world's most noted experts of Northwest Coast Indian art—Lee Wallace, a fifth-generation Haida carver, was selected to carve the pole. Amazingly, several years after Wallace was hired for this project, Dr. Scherer and Bill Holm provided information that showed that Lee's great-grandfather, Dwight Wallace, had carved the original Golden Hill totem pole. What a wonderful coincidence that the carver chosen for the project was related to the carver of the original pole!

The site on which the totem pole had stood wouldn't be forgotten, either. Early on in the project, a historical marker was approved by the Indiana State Historical Bureau and placed at the original site of the pole in Golden Hill. The First Lady of Indiana, Susan Bayh, Golden Hill residents, and members of the Indianapolis historical, civic, museum, and arts communities were present for the marker's dedication. A few years later, a stone and bronze monument that pictured the totem and told its history was also placed at the Golden Hill location.

An Indiana State Historical Bureau marker (right) and a stone and bronze monument mark the original Indianapolis site of the totem pole in Golden Hill.

NOW IT was time to re-create the original pole in all its beauty and significance. It would be done by Lee Wallace in Alaska and then brought to Indianapolis and the Eiteljorg Museum. In a true community effort, individuals, foundations, and corp- orations generously contributed money for the pole's carving and transportation costs. For example, the Cape Fox Native Corporation of Ketchikan donated the four- hundred-year-old cedar tree. Students from Nora Elementary School in Indian- apolis, who learned about Native American culture, took the totem pole to their hearts and raised more than two thousand dollars from walkathons. Meanwhile, local newspaper, magazine, and television coverage resulted in public awareness of the project. Finally, the Lilly Endowment provided support for a Public Broadcasting Service documentary on the forgotten pole's history and recreation.

Before carving, the original red western cedar log was forty feet long and weighed about eighty-five hundred pounds.

Lee Wallace planed the log with a chain saw to remove the outer layer of sapwood and to create the desired diameter of the log to be carved for the Indianapolis pole.

LEE WALLACE began carving the totem pole in 1994. Working on other projects as well, he completed the Indianapolis pole over a two-year period. Author Richard Feldman and his family made two trips to Alaska during this time to view the progress in the carving and for the filming of the PBS documentary "Tale of a Totem." The filming took place at Sitka National Historical Park and at the carving studio in the native village of Saxman, near Ketchikan. Wallace chose native Alaskan Edwin DeWitt as his assistant carver for the Indianapolis project, and together they worked on every detail of the totem figures. Many people from Indianapolis visited Saxman during those two years, and would send Feldman photographs of the pole at various stages of completion.

A paper pattern is created to outline the design to be carved.

Lee Wallace works on the Indianapolis pole with an adze.

Partially carved sections of the Indianapolis pole show the characters of a watchman (right) and a Wasgo (below).

Lee Wallace carves
the basic design on
the Indianapolis pole
with a chain saw
(left), and assistant
carver Edwin DeWitt
carves detail with a
woodworking knife.

WHEN THE carving was nearly complete, the Mayflower Corporation donated the cost of shipping the totem pole by barge from Ketchikan, Alaska, to Seattle, Washington, and then by truck across the country to Indianapolis. Away the pole went. During the week before the pole raising, Lee Wallace completed the final touches on the pole, on-site at the Eiteljorg Museum.

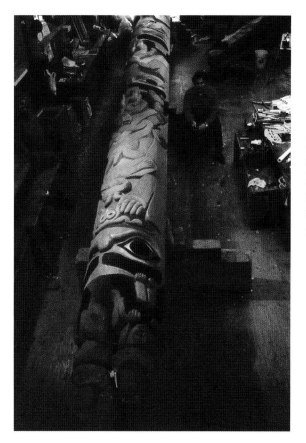

Lee Wallace poses proudly with the almost-finished Golden Hill pole in his carving studio at Saxman Village near Ketchikan, Alaska, just before shipping to Indianapolis. (Photo by unknown Ketchikan photographer)

The final carving and painting are completed on-site at the Eiteljorg Museum during the week before the pole raising. (Courtesy of Eiteljorg Museum)

BECAUSE THE totem pole re-created the crest figures of the Yeltatzie family, the native owners of the original pole, the museum requested their permission to raise the new pole in Indianapolis. On April 13, 1996, with their permission, the traditional pole raising finally occurred on the front lawn of the Eiteljorg Museum. In attendance were several members of the Parry family; the carver, Lee Wallace, and his family; representatives of the Yeltatzie family from Ketchikan, and Masset, British Columbia, Canada; and local members and leaders of the Miami Nation of Indians of Indiana. Just before the pole was raised, Lee Wallace gave author Richard Feldman the honor of making the last strike on the pole with an adze.

Tlingit elder Tom Abbot came to Indianapolis to attend the Eiteljorg Museum totem pole raising. (Courtesy Shawn Spence)

THE POLE was erected by more than one hundred volunteers who pulled on ropes under the direction of Tlingit clan leader Wayne Shields from Ketchikan. Adding to the prestige of the celebration were Haida and Tlingit elders, the Cape Fox Dancers, and the Haida Star Dancers. They sang songs and performed traditional dances for the four thousand-plus people who attended the event. After a dedication speech by Indiana's then-Lieutenant Governor (and later Governor) Frank O'Bannon, the chief of the Indiana Miami tribe and Mary Yeltatzie Swanson offered traditional blessings.

The Eiteljorg Museum totem pole lies in its trench in readiness for the raising ceremony.

The totem pole raising at the Eiteljorg Museum was accomplished in the traditional way, with more than a hundred people pulling on ropes. The crane was used only as a safety measure.

Tlingit clan leader Wayne Shields (in hat) directs the pole raising, commanding each tug of the ropes with a beat of the drum. Members of the Yeltatzie family (between Shields and the pole) and the Parry family (to the right of Shields) look on. (Courtesy Shawn Spence)

WHEN THE pole was up, Lee Wallace invited his assistant carver, Edwin DeWitt, and the author to perform the carver's dance with him around the pole with adzes in hand. More traditional singing, dancing, and story-telling continued outside for some time. The dancers also invited other honored guests to participate in the chief's dance, and Lee Wallace told the Golden Hill totem pole's mythical story of Wasgo, the sea monster.

OF COURSE, the museum held a potlatch that evening! Everyone feasted on smoked Alaskan king salmon and other Northwest foods. More traditional dancing and singing, including the raven and eagle dances, continued on into the evening. Dozens of natives and invited guests danced in their button robes (also called button blankets) to the beat of hand-held drums. Various people involved with the project gave presentations and speeches. Natives presented gifts to honored guests and the museum gave everyone commemorative buttons to take home to remember the pole raising. Hundreds of Indianapolis people from all walks of life joined in friendship with the native Alaskan guests to celebrate and honor the totem pole that evening. These events were unusual happenings for a typical Midwestern community. The Northwest Coast had come to Indianapolis! And the totem pole had returned to its long-time home.

Tlingit and Haida dancers perform at the Eiteljorg Museum totem pole raising. The carver's daughter, Kara Wallace (center), was among the dancers and singers.

Mary Yeltatzie Swanson, granddaughter of Yeltatzie, the native owner of the original Indianapolis totem pole, greeted the crowd at the celebration.

The potlatch celebration after the pole raising continued well into the evening inside the museum, and included more ceremonial dances by Wayne Shields (left) and Edwin DeWitt.

Assistant carver Edwin DeWitt performs the carver's dance.

John Wallace, son of carver Lee Wallace, attended the ceremony dressed in a traditional carved-wood headdress and button robe.

A group of Haida in Klinkwan, Alaska, ca. 1903. Dwight Wallace (front row, right), carver of the original Indianapolis totem pole and great-grandfather of Eiteljorg totem pole carver Lee Wallace, holds a Chilkat blanket on his lap. (Courtesy Yale Collection of Western Americana, Beinecke Rare Book and Manuscript Library)

THE CHANGNG APPEARANCE OF THE GOLDEN HILL TOTEM POLE

BILL HOLM helped determine that the pole seen in Figure 1 (page 62) was indeed the Golden Hill totem pole as it originally stood in Alaska in 1901 before being taken by Brady. But this pole looks different from the pole shown in Figure 2 (also on page 62) when it later stood in Golden Hill. How could it be the Golden Hill totem pole and yet not be an exact match? Can you spot the differences between the two totem poles?

How and why did these changes occur? Remember that the pole broke in several pieces when Brady collected it in Alaska. Brady brought down a crew of native Alaskan carvers to the St. Louis Fair to repair, recarve, and paint portions of the totem poles. Evidently, the Golden Hill pole was altered from its original appearance during the repair of the rotted and broken areas when used by Dick Crane. The original native Alaskan owner, Yeltatzie, had two almost identical poles. The Yeltatzie mate pole is seen in Figure 3 (page 63). Because that totem pole is thought to be almost identical to the original appearance of the Golden Hill pole, it was used as the model for the new pole at the Eiteljorg Museum.

Figure 1: The Golden Hill totem pole at its original location in Alaska, 1901. (Courtesy of National Anthropological Archives, Smithsonian Institution neg. # 92-7098)

Figure 2: The Golden Hill totem pole in Indianapolis, 1907.

Figure 3: The Yeltatzie mate pole, Howkan, Alaska, 1901. This pole was also owned by Yeltatzie and carved by Dwight Wallace. This pole is an excellent example of a house frontal totem pole. (Smithsonian Institution neg # SI4317)

The Watchman Figures who protect
the clan house and village

The Man in the Skin of Wasgo,
the Sea Monster

Spirit of the Wind Bird (not in the story)

The Trap with Effigy Figure of Unknown Animal

The Mother-in-Law

Wasgo, the Sea Monster

The Man

A Bear, the crest figure of Yeltatzie's clan

Photograph by Dan Axler

FIGURES OF THE
GOLDEN HILL TOTEM POLE
AT THE EITELJORG MUSEUM

THE MYTH TOLD BY THE GOLDEN HILL TOTEM POLE

The story of Wasgo, the sea monster.
Are you wondering what is the
actual story the totem tells?
Here it is . . .

ONCE A LONG time ago, a man fell in love with a girl from an important, wealthy family in the village. He wanted to marry the girl, but her parents would not agree to the marriage because they felt that he was not worthy. Finally, they gave their permission for the marriage, but only if he agreed to work very hard for them. Although the man worked all the time, almost as a slave, he could never seem to please his mother-in-law.

One day, the man, feeling very frustrated and sad, went away to think things over. He was determined to find a way to prove himself to his wife's family. He walked into the woods to the lake near the village, where the lake flowed into the sea. There he set a big V-shaped trap by splitting a cedar tree, so he could catch Wasgo, the sea monster. He knew that he would have great powers if he killed and skinned Wasgo and placed the skin over himself. However, he also knew he had to be very careful of one thing: he must always be out of the sea monster's skin and back to the village before the raven cawed in the morning. So the man set the trap, and he caught, killed, and skinned the sea monster.

At that time there was great hunger in the village, so the man decided one night to bring a salmon to the village for everyone to eat. In the skin of Wasgo, he swam and got a large salmon and placed the fish on the beach at his mother-in-law's house. Night after night, the man would bring salmon or halibut to her house, and the next morning she would find it and share the food with those in the village. The people began to think that the mother-in-law was a person with supernatural powers, a *shaman*, with the ability to have spirits bring food to the village. She soon began to act like a shaman with the power to make these things happen. Wearing a shaman's headdress, each day the mother-in-law would shake her puffin rattles and predict that the next morning there would be a seal or a sea lion on the beach for the village to eat. And each night the man would go to the sea and deliver whatever she wanted. The more credit the mother-in-law received and the more important she felt, the meaner she was to the man. But he said nothing about what he was doing.

Finally, the mother-in-law said that in the morning there would be a killer whale on the beach at her house. The man caught a whale, and although it was very difficult to carry to the village, it was there as she wished. The next day the mother-in-law predicted that there would be two whales on the shore the next morning, and again the man went to the sea to get what she had foretold. However, the two whales were too much for the man to carry. He was not able to return with them to the village before the raven cawed, and so the man died.

That morning, the mother-in-law and all the people of the

village saw the man in the skin of the sea monster lying dead on the beach next to the two killer whales. They knew then that all along it had been the man and not his mother-in-law who had provided food for the village. The woman died in shame, and the people honored the man as a very great person.

The man had instructed his wife that if he should die, she was to remove his body from Wasgo's skin and place it under a tree near the shore of the lake. She did exactly that. She loved her husband very much, so every evening she went to the tree where his body lay to be with him. One day, the sea monster rose out of the lake before her. She was not afraid because she could feel that the spirit of her husband was within the sea monster. She took its hand and together they swam to the bottom of the lake and live there to this day in Wasgo's beautiful house.

Epilogue

The raising of the new totem pole at the Eiteljorg Museum in Indianapolis brings full circle a story that began in Alaska more than a hundred and fifty years ago. The pole as it originally stood in a faraway island native village in southeast Alaska traditionally represented family and community. When it stood in Indianapolis after the 1904 World's Fair, although in a totally new and different setting, it again symbolized family and community. This time it was an important part of the Parry family and the neighborhood of Golden Hill. And now, as the pole stands at the Eiteljorg Museum, it once again represents family and community. It is a visual symbol of the community spirit and support that made the creation of the new totem pole possible. It also represents that grand day, ninety-one years after the original pole arrived in Indianapolis, when the Parry, Yeltatzie, and Wallace families all met and united as one American family.

During the pole raising in Indianapolis, something very special occurred that was hardly noticed by the thousands in attendance. Mary Freda Parry, ninety-seven years old and the last of the Parry family in Indianapolis, arrived and was greeted by the Yeltatzies, carver Lee Wallace, and other Haida and Tlingit natives. The

Yeltatzies honored Mrs. Parry by presenting her with a red button robe. With tears running down her face, she looked up and said, "This means we have a connection, doesn't it?" At that moment, there was an understanding that although separated by thousands of miles, cultural differences, and years of history, they all had a very important connection indeed. They were united together by *their* totem pole in friendship and pride.

Back home again in Indiana, the pole is more than a work of art. It is a visual symbol of traditions and history that ties together families, diverse cultures, communities, and new friends across the American continent. Today, when you go to the Eiteljorg Museum, stand quietly next to the totem pole. Listen very closely. The totem pole whispers the message of family, community, and friendship.

Young John Wallace (second from left) and friends at the Eiteljorg Museum Totem Pole raising.

Through exhibitions, performances, and hands-on workshops with artists, the Eiteljorg Museum of American Indian and Western Art immerses visitors in the American West and Native America — the only museum in the Midwest to offer this combination. Temporary and traveling exhibitions explore the many cultures of North America, from the past as well as the present.